The Stolen Signs

A Southside Sluggers Baseball Mystery

Created by Glenn Lewis and Gail Tuchman
Written by Steven Otfinoski
Illustrated by Bert Dodson

LITTLE SIMON
Published by Simon & Schuster
New York ♦ London ♦ Toronto ♦ Sydney ♦ Tokyo ♦ Singapore

LITTLE SIMON

Simon & Schuster Building, Rockefeller Center, 1230 Avenue of the
Americas, New York, New York 10020 Text copyright © 1992 by
Glenn Lewis and Gail Tuchman. Illustrations copyright © 1992 by
Bert Dodson. All rights reserved including the right of reproduction in
whole or in part in any form.
LITTLE SIMON and colophon are trademarks of Simon & Schuster.
Designed by Lucille Chomowicz.
The text of this book is set in Stempel Garamond.
The illustrations were done in black ink.
Also available in a SIMON & SCHUSTER BOOKS FOR YOUNG READERS hardcover
edition. Series conceived and text produced by Book Smart Inc.
Manufactured in the United States of America.
10 9 8 7 6 5 4 3 2 1   (pbk) 10 9 8 7 6 5 4 3 2 1
ISBN: 0-671-72926-8   ISBN: 0-671-72930-6 (pbk)

Contents

The Stolen Signs

1 Mauled by the Mudsharks

"Safe!" cried the first-base umpire.

The Mudsharks hitter stood up and dusted himself off at first base. He smiled, and for good reason. His team was winning, 3–2, with two players now on base and less than an inning left in the game.

Pitcher Zach Langlin of the Southside Sluggers felt a sinking feeling in the pit of his stomach. Zach only experienced this feeling on two occasions. One was when he was about to take a test he hadn't studied for. The other time was when he was losing a ball game he should've been winning.

Zach turned and looked over his right shoulder at the other Mudshark on third base. The kid was greedily eyeing home plate. It was beginning to rattle the pitcher.

Catcher Andy West picked up on Zach's feelings.

He called for time out and strode up to the pitcher's mound.

"Take it easy, Zach," Andy said in a soft but encouraging voice. "Don't get so tense. Remember these are the Mudsharks of the Lotus Pines Youth Baseball League you're pitching to, not the New York Yankees."

"Tell *them* that," replied Zach. "They're the worst team in the league, so why aren't they living up to their reputation?"

"You mean living *down* to it, don't you?" replied Andy.

Zach frowned. He was supposed to be the team comic, not Andy. No one seemed to be doing what was expected—not Andy, not the Mudsharks. It was really throwing Zach off his game.

"Look, just relax and keep those pitches coming in," said Andy. "The next batter is Billy Butler. He'll be an easy out. Then one more to go and we get another crack at it. All we need is a couple of runs to show the Mudsharks who's the big fish on this field."

In the last inning of the game Andy's words sounded overly confident to Zach, but he just nodded. Leave it to Andy to put the best face on things, even in an impossible situation.

Andy trotted back to the plate and Billy Butler sheepishly stepped up to bat. Zach couldn't help but smile. If the Mudsharks were the worst team around, Billy was a top contender for the Worst Hitter award.

Zach called him the "Fly Swatter" because Billy swung at the ball like he was swatting at flies, with the same negative results.

Zach stared with steely eyes at Billy's pale, plump face. He looked for the signal from Andy. The catcher carefully extended one finger down from his crouched position behind the plate. It was the signal for a fastball. Zach nodded slightly, pressed his tongue against his upper lip, and wound up for the pitch. The ball whizzed toward home plate.

"Strike one!" cried the umpire behind the plate.

Billy look slightly dazed. He hadn't moved a muscle. Zach wondered if he had even seen the ball come by. Andy tossed the ball back to Zach and gave him the signal for another fast pitch.

Billy choked up on the bat and tried to look determined. It wasn't a very convincing act. Zach gripped the ball and delivered the pitch.

The "Fly Swatter" lived up to his name. Billy swung wildly at the speeding ball, never coming near it.

"Strike two!" exclaimed the umpire. Zach's stomach was feeling decidedly better.

This time Andy extended two fingers downward from his left hand. It was a signal for a slow ball. Zach smiled ever so slightly. He approved of the mix in pitches. Billy would be tensed up for another fastball and be completely thrown by the slow pitch.

Zach was careful not to telegraph his pitch. He gave Billy the same steely stare and made the same big

windup as before. But when the ball left his hand, it was at half the speed.

What happened next, however, was even more unexpected. To Zach's amazement, Billy Butler was ready and waiting for the pitch. He swung squarely at the ball and made solid contact.

It wasn't a great hit. Billy was no Babe Ruth. But he didn't have to be. The ball flew into center field. Second baseman Luis Diaz made a great effort to catch it, but missed the ball by inches. Right fielder Rachel Langlin, Zach's older sister, retrieved the ball and threw it home. But too late.

The Mudshark on third had slid home moments before. Andy quickly shot the ball back to third baseman Michelle Brooks. But the fast-footed Mudshark on first slid into third just before the ball reached Michelle.

Meanwhile, Billy Butler had managed to hotfoot it to first. He stood there grinning like a kid in a toothpaste commercial. *I'd grin too, if I'd just had my first base hit in fifteen games*, thought Zach.

He looked up at the scoreboard, which now read 4–2. Zach could feel his stomach starting to slide down toward his feet again. He glanced at Andy, who only shook his head. The next batter stepped brightly up to the plate.

This time Andy gave the signal for an outside fastball—one finger extended down and the catcher's mitt positioned away from the batter. He knew the batter was a sucker for an outside pitch.

Zach delivered the pitch as signaled. But if the batter had a weakness for an outside ball, he didn't show it now. The bat struck the ball with a crack and the ball sailed into right field. It fell just short of Rachel Langlin, who picked it up on one hop and threw it to second. Billy was caught between bases and tagged out. The player on third, however, slid into home a moment before the ball reached Andy's waiting mitt.

"Safe!" cried the umpire.

The next batter hit a high fly that Seth Bradigan, the team's hot new left fielder, caught easily. It was the Sluggers' turn at bat, but the damage had been done.

Seth, also the Sluggers' best hitter, slammed a line-drive double to left field. Unfortunately, he was still at second when the final Slugger struck out.

The game was over. The Mudsharks, the Southside Sluggers' arch-rivals, had trounced the not-so-great but recently up-and-coming Sluggers, 5–2. And they scored all five of their runs in the final three innings—when the Sluggers' best pitcher, Zach Langlin, was on the mound.

Center fielder Susan Stein threw her glove down in disgust. Shortstop Ernie Peters pulled his cap over his face, and first baseman Marty Franklin kicked the juice cooler.

Coach Terwilliger tried to cheer the Sluggers with some words of encouragement, but they had little effect on the team's spirits.

"Nice throw, Sis," Zach said to Rachel, trying to

sound cheerful. "You did a good job picking off that runner."

"Thanks, little brother," replied Rachel. "Nice pitching. I just don't know what got into those Mudsharks."

"They just had a lucky day, that's all," piped up Andy. "It happens to everyone once in a while."

"Nobody's *that* lucky," said Zach. "Especially not Billy Butler."

"Don't worry," said Seth. "We're going up against those guys in exactly three weeks and next time we'll shove them right back down where they belong—in the cellar!"

Zach laughed along with the others, but his heart wasn't in it. He had pitched as good a three innings as he was capable of, against a team they always expected to beat.

All the rest of that day Zach couldn't get Billy Butler's face out of his mind. He kept seeing that cool, confident expression Billy wore when the slow ball came toward him. It was as if he knew it was coming before it even left Zach's hand. But how? That question kept Zach Langlin awake half the night.

2 Who Stole the Signs?

The next afternoon, after practice, Zach, Rachel, Andy, and Seth were sitting in the Southside Ice Cream Shop, located in the Southside section of Lotus Pines.

Zach and Rachel's father, Mr. Langlin, was the team sponsor and owner of the shop. In fact, he had designed the green-and-orange team uniform to match two of his more bizarre ice-cream flavors—Pickleberry Sundae and Orang-u-tang Chip.

"I just can't understand it," muttered Zach. "It's as if those Mudsharks knew exactly what I was going to pitch every time."

"Come on, Zach," said Seth. "You're beginning to sound like a broken record. You had an off day and the Mudsharks had a lucky one. Drop it."

Zach took a long sip of his Orang-u-tang Chip soda.

"But that's just it," he went on. "I *didn't* have an off day. My pitching was the best it's been in weeks. Just ask Andy."

Andy looked up at his friends from his half-finished banana split. As the peacemaker of the group, he wasn't anxious to get drawn into an argument. "Zach was pitching very well," he admitted slowly. "His off-speed pitches and fastballs were right on target. The Mudsharks just seemed to be hitting everything he could throw them."

"It doesn't make sense," said Zach. "If we had been playing against the Toyshop Tigers or the Rocket Raiders, I could accept what happened. But the *Mudsharks* . . . no way! There's got to be some other explanation."

Rachel wiped some Boysenberry Bash ice cream from her mouth. Zach eyed Rachel's ice cream. If there was one flavor Zach couldn't stand, it was Boysenberry Bash!

Rachel gave her bright red hair a toss. "Well, let's look at this thing logically," she said. "It occurs to me there are four possible explanations here."

Zach rolled his baby blue eyes upward. "Okay, Professor," he said. "Let's hear them. Just try to keep the college words to a minimum so us poor elementary school kids can understand you."

"All right," said Rachel, choosing to ignore her brother. "One, the Mudsharks have miraculously turned into a first-rate team overnight."

"Impossible!" cried Seth.

"Okay," smiled Rachel. "I think we can safely rule that one out. Besides, the Mudsharks' fielding was as bad as ever. Our poor hitting in the game was due more to our own mistakes than to any great defensive plays they made. It doesn't make sense that the Mudsharks would suddenly become heavy hitters while remaining rotten fielders."

"Agreed," chimed in Andy. "Let's hear number two."

"Number two," continued Rachel, "there's the matter of luck that Seth brought up. I can see luck accounting for a good inning, but not half of the game."

"I suppose you're right," sighed Seth. "Even though they didn't score against Robin Hayes in the first three innings, they belted Zach all over from the fourth through the sixth."

"Which brings us to explanation number three," Rachel went on. "If the Mudsharks' hitting streak was due, as my brother insists, to their knowing what Zach was pitching before every pitch, it could mean they are masters of *mental telepathy*."

"There you go!" cried Zach. "I knew you couldn't talk for two minutes without dropping in a zinger of a word!"

"Telepathy is communication between minds by means other than normal sensory channels," explained Rachel.

"Are you trying to say that the Mudsharks are . . . *mind readers?*" asked Seth.

"Impossible!" replied Andy.

"I know," agreed Rachel. "Anyway, they'd have to be super geniuses to cut through the fog in Zach's head and read *his* mind."

"Very funny," shot back her brother. "Remind me to laugh at that — oh, sometime next week."

"Which brings us to the fourth and last possibility," said Rachel, again ignoring Zach, "that the Mudsharks are somehow stealing our signals as Andy is flashing them to the pitcher."

"That's it!" exclaimed Zach, nearly knocking over his soda glass. "They're stealing our signs! I take back everything I've said about you. They don't call you Sherlock for nothing."

"It makes sense," agreed Seth. "The Mudsharks are just desperate enough — and low enough — to try something like that. It would explain why Robin did so well in the beginning — and why Zach got bombed at the end. It could've taken three innings to steal our signs."

"Just a minute," broke in Andy. "I don't see how they could steal my signals. I always keep my mitt over my left knee to hide the signs from the batter and the third-base coach. And I'm careful to keep my right knee in front of the left one so the first-base coach can't see anything and pass it on to the batter."

"Nobody's accusing you of being sloppy with your signals, Andy," said Zach. "Maybe the Mudsharks have some clever way of stealing the signs that we haven't thought of."

"Like what?" asked Seth. "Tiny reflecting mirrors?"

"That's one possibility," said Rachel. "Or maybe they planted a spy in the stands to see Andy's signals and then relay them to the batter."

Andy shook his head. "That wouldn't work," he said. "How could someone in the stands see the signals and feed them to the batter at the same time? It's impossible. They'd have to be two places at once."

"This is getting awfully confusing," sighed Seth. "The mental telepathy bit sounds almost as believable. Anyway, do we really think the Mudsharks are smart enough to work out such a scheme?"

"Maybe their coach worked it out for them," suggested Rachel.

"No," argued Andy, "Coach Terwilliger wouldn't try to pull a stunt like that just to win a game, and I don't think any other coach in the league would either."

The others had to admit it seemed unlikely.

"There's one other possibility we haven't thought about," said Seth. "Maybe someone was sending the signals to the Mudsharks—not from the stands, but from the field."

"How could that happen?" asked Andy. "The only ones in the field when the Mudsharks were up at bat were our own teammates."

Suddenly there was a long silence as the other three stared at Seth.

"Are you saying maybe one of the Sluggers is a . . . spy, a traitor?" said Rachel.

Seth looked a little shamefaced. "I'm only saying it's a possibility," he said. "We've got to cover all the bases, so to speak, if we're going to get to the bottom of this mystery. Don't we?"

"Okay," agreed Rachel reluctantly. "Let's consider it. Is there anyone on our team who'd have any reason for wanting to hurt us and see us lose?"

The four Sluggers thought for a long moment.

"Well," said Zach at last, "Susan Stein was pretty upset when Michelle was moved to third base and Sue had to stay in the outfield. Maybe she wants to get revenge on the whole team for that."

"No way," replied Rachel. "Susan may have been a little ticked at the time, but she'd never help another team beat us."

"I agree," said Andy. "Anyway, how could she see my signals from center field, let alone pass them along to the batter?"

"Both of them would have to have X-ray vision," said Seth.

"Okay, okay," replied Zach. "So maybe we shouldn't be trying to put the blame on teammates. But *somebody* had to be helping the Mudsharks get those signals."

"I have an idea" said Andy.

"Shoot," said Rachel.

"We can't be sure anyone is stealing our signals," Andy reasoned. "But there is one way to make sure no

one can use them against us again. We just ask Coach Terwilliger to change the signs completely before our next game against the Tigers on Saturday."

"Great idea!" exclaimed Zach. "If the Mudsharks stole the signs and passed them on to the Tigers, they'll be worthless in the next game!"

"I'll call the coach tonight and explain it all to him," said Andy. "And I'll call Robin Hayes first to let her know what's going on."

"Uh, it might be a good idea, Andy, if only the coach, you, Robin, and I know what the new signals are," suggested Zach.

Rachel's bright blue eyes grew wide and her red freckles looked like they were about to pop right off her face.

"Are you suggesting your own sister might be a spy?" she demanded.

"Of course not," replied Zach. "But everyone knows what a loose set of lips you have. You just might spill the whole thing to—"

Zach never finished his sentence. For at that moment Rachel *did* spill something—the remainder of her Boysenberry Bash ice cream (the flavor Zach hated) right into his Orang-u-tang Chip soda.

3 The Man with the Camera

Coach Terwilliger was a little surprised when Andy called that night to ask that he change the pitching signs. Andy skirted around the issue of sign stealing. Instead he said Zach felt the old signs were getting a little rusty. It didn't sound all that convincing. So the catcher was relieved when the coach himself brought up the real issue.

"Andy," said Coach Terwilliger in his gravelly voice, "do you think the Mudsharks have stolen our signals?"

Andy thought a long moment before answering. "I don't know, Coach," he replied, "but a bunch of us were discussing it this afternoon. There's something strange about how the Mudsharks beat us."

"This 'bunch' being you, Rachel, Seth, and Zach, right?" asked the coach.

"You got it, Coach," answered Andy with a grin. Not much got past Coach Terwilliger.

"Then it looks like you budding private eyes have found yourselves a mystery to solve," said the coach good-humoredly.

"We're not sure yet," said Andy. "But if the signs are changed before our next game, and Zach's and Robin's pitches don't get hit all over the ballpark by the Tigers, we'll know there is no sign stealing going on anymore. We'll have stopped it."

"And what if our pitches do get hit all over the place?" the coach asked.

Andy sighed. "Then we'll know we've got a real problem on our hands."

"I don't know if there's any stealing going on or not," said the coach. "But if changing the signs will make you and the pitchers feel better and play your best, I'm willing to try it."

"Thanks, Coach. That's all we wanted," said Andy.

"I'll see you, Zach, and Robin on the practice field at three-thirty Thursday afternoon," said the coach. "Then you can try out your new signals on your teammates at batting practice at four."

Andy thanked the coach, hung up, and immediately dialed Zach and Robin to tell them the good news.

On Thursday Coach Terwilliger gave all-new signals to his pitchers and catcher. A fastball became a closed fist. A slow ball was now an open palm and a pitchout was a wiggle of the fingers. There was no sign for a curveball because the pitch was not permitted by the Lotus Pines Youth Baseball League.

The coach had the threesome practice the new signals over and over. He knew they would be harder for Zach and Robin to read than the extended fingers signals.

By the time their teammates showed up for batting practice, the pitchers and Andy felt confident about the new signals and were anxious to try them out. One by one, Zach struck out the batters he faced. His pitching arm felt stronger with every ball he threw.

"Think we're ready for the Tigers?" whispered Andy as they finished practice.

Zach tugged at his cap and smiled. "We're gonna knock the stripes off them," he whispered back.

"You guys cook up some new signals?" asked a familiar voice.

Zach turned sharply to see Susan Stein standing nearby.

Susan narrowed her green eyes and her mouth went a little crooked. "What's goin' on?" she asked. "Some kind of top-secret signal or something?"

"What makes you think we have new signals?" Andy asked suspiciously.

"I got here early and saw you guys and Robin working with the coach," she explained. "It's not unusual to switch signals when a team isn't playing well."

"We're playing just fine," replied Zach, defensively. "As for the signals, they're no secret."

"Then why are you two acting like a couple of clams?" persisted Susan.

"It's just bad luck to talk about things like that before a game," spoke up Andy quickly. *When in need of an excuse,* he thought, *always fall back on superstition. No athletes are more superstitious than baseball players.*

The suspicious expression on Susan's face didn't change. "Have it your way," she said. "I just hope whatever you've cooked up helps us win on Saturday."

Before either Zach or Andy could say another word, Susan had turned and walked off the field.

"Who does she think she is?" said Zach.

"Well, you have to admit we weren't exactly friendly," said Andy.

"Maybe not," confessed Zach, "but what was I supposed to do? Tell her what the new signs were? Maybe Rachel's right and she's no spy, but we don't know for sure."

Andy nodded grimly. "Let's just hope all goes well on Saturday and we don't have to suspect anyone of anything."

Saturday was a perfect spring day, with clear blue skies and not a cloud to be seen. Every player in the league looked forward to a Saturday game. It was the weekend, with no school the next day to take their minds off the game. Also, there was always a good crowd in the stands. The grandstands of Bloom Field were filled with anxious relatives and baseball-hungry kids—all ready to cheer their favorite team on to victory. Nothing brings out the fighting spirit of a baseball team like a cheering crowd of eager fans.

The Sluggers took to the field against the Toyshop Tigers as the game began. Zach loosened up his arm with a few pitches to Andy. He then stepped off the rubber and looked around at the spectators. The coach had decided to begin this game with his ace pitcher. Zach noticed a man snapping pictures with a professional-looking camera that had a zoom lens. *He must be from the* Lotus Times, Zach thought. *It's the only newspaper in the town of Lotus Pines that covers our league.*

Zach self-consciously put his tongue into his mouth and smiled in the direction of the zoom lens. It wouldn't do to have his picture in the local paper with his big tongue sticking out. It was a bad habit that his sister and other teammates were always teasing him about. It had also earned him the nickname Zach "The Tongue" Langlin. Although Zach preferred to think he got the nickname for his reputation as the team's king wisecracker.

The first Tiger stepped up to the plate. Zach had no trouble striking her out—and the next player as well. Then, the Tigers called a totally unexpected time-out.

Seven or eight Tigers ran out from their dugout to talk to the player who was about to bat. They formed a big huddle, made plenty of hand gestures, and whispered a whole lot of instructions. Surprisingly, their coach was not part of the huddle.

Finally, the third batter went to the plate. He took two hard-thrown strikes. Then he wacked a base hit off the only off-speed pitch Zach threw. It was as if he knew exactly when it was coming.

The next batter let two inside fastballs go by. He then teed off of a fastball right down the middle of the plate. It rocketed all the way to the left-field fence for a stand-up triple.

Zach started to get that old sinking feeling in the pit of his stomach. Suddenly, the Tigers were clued into everything he was trying to do. It was almost as if Andy were signaling to the Tigers rather than to his own pitcher.

But how could this be? The signals were new and Zach *was* pitching well. There was no way anybody could have picked up on the signs so soon—even a pretty good team like the Tigers.

Yet the Toyshop Tigers were picking out pitches like a bunch of All-Stars. By the second inning, Zach's confidence was crumbling. Even Seth's two-run homer didn't help. The Tigers already had seven runs of their own. And the game was turning into a romp.

"Buck up, little brother," said Rachel, as they came in from the field in the bottom of the third. "You did your best."

"Sure," said Zach, with little conviction. It wasn't just the runs that bothered him. The Tigers were hitting his best pitches consistently. The new signals didn't seem to be making any difference at all.

"I'm being as careful as I can, Zach," said Andy, as they sat down on the bench to wait their turn at bat. "There's no way anyone in the infield could be picking up the signals I'm giving you."

Zach patted his friend reassuringly on the shoulder. "I know that, Andy," he said. "But something funny's going on. I just wish I knew what it was."

Zach's eyes traveled back to the stands. The man with the camera was intently reloading it with a new roll of film.

"Is that guy with the newspaper?" he asked the other players on the bench.

"No," replied first baseman Marty Franklin. "The sports reporter for the *Lotus Times* is a younger guy. Besides, they only send a photographer over to cover the championship games."

Zach kept staring at the man, who looked about forty and was dressed in a business suit. Rachel and Andy looked at the man too, with growing curiosity.

"I wonder who he is," asked Rachel.

"I don't know," confessed shortstop Ernie Peters. "But he must like to watch us play. He was at the game against the Mudsharks, too."

Zach's eyes grew wide and he turned to Ernie. "Are you sure he was there?" he asked.

"Positive," replied Ernie. "You couldn't miss him with that big camera."

"You mean he was taking pictures at the last game, too?" asked Rachel excitedly.

"Every inning," answered Ernie.

"Maybe he's somebody's father or uncle or something," ventured Andy.

"Maybe," said Zach thoughtfully.

Rachel was about to say something but thought better of it. She would save her suspicions until she was alone with her brother and two friends. It wouldn't do to bring up the question of signal stealing with the rest of the team in the middle of a game. They needed to concentrate.

Susan Stein struck out and it was back to the field for the Sluggers. Robin Hayes replaced Zach on the mound and Andy took his position behind home plate. Andy looked up at the stands and saw the well-dressed man, camera in hand, looking directly at him through the zoom lens.

Is he taking pictures of my signals to the pitcher? Andy wondered. Before he could answer his own question, his eyes traveled over to another person in the stands. It was a girl wearing a floppy red hat. She was looking intently at the field through a pair of large binoculars.

Andy felt cold sweat break out on his forehead. *This is crazy*, he thought. *I better watch it, or I'm going to start supposing everyone is out to get our signals!*

"Are you ready to play ball, catcher?" asked the umpire dryly.

"Yes, sir!" said Andy, bringing his catcher's mask down over his face.

"Then stop daydreaming," said the ump.

The game ended with the final score Tigers 13, Sluggers 6. Zach had given up nine runs the first three innings. Robin did a bit better by allowing only four runs in the last half of the game.

"Maybe they got tired of scoring runs at the end," said Zach in disgust. "Or maybe they just started to feel guilty."

4 Three Suspects

"There's no doubt about it anymore," said Rachel grimly. "Somebody's stealing our signs and we've got to find out who it is and how they're doing it."

She looked around Seth's downstairs den at the three troubled faces of her friends. After the game, the four had decided to meet at Seth's instead of at the Southside Ice Cream Shop. They all felt they needed more privacy to discuss the troubling matter before them.

"The Tigers might have beaten us, anyway, but not the way they did today," said Zach, agreeing with his sister. "They were prepared for every pitch I threw them. Last time we played them, my fastball struck out one batter after another. This time, they were ready and waiting. They knew our signs, all right."

"The question is, How, Zach?" piped up Andy, sitting in Seth's plastic beanbag chair. "Nobody knew about the new signs but Coach Terwilliger, Robin, you, and me."

"We don't know that for sure," interrupted the pitcher. "There is one other person who may have overheard us talking about the signs with the coach."

"Who?" asked Rachel anxiously.

Zach told his sister and Seth about their run-in at practice with Susan Stein.

"You can't pin this on Susan just because she happened to be there," argued Rachel. "There is nothing reprehensible about a coincidence."

"Please translate," groaned Zach.

"You can't blame somebody for an accident," cried Rachel, in no mood for her brother's humor.

"It might have been an innocent accident," reasoned Seth, sprawled out on an overstuffed sofa. "And it also might have been on purpose. I don't like accusing Susan any more than you do, Rach, but you have to admit, she has been behaving kind of strange lately."

Rachel sighed sadly. "I know what you mean. Every time I try to talk to her she hardly has a thing to say. We used to get along great and now there's some kind of wall between us."

"A guilty conscience, maybe?" offered Zach.

"Okay," admitted Rachel. "It looks like we've got our first suspect. I just hope we're all wrong about her."

With that, Rachel grabbed a piece of chalk and started to write on a small chalkboard on the wall. She made three columns. One column was headed

SUSPECT, a second OPPORTUNITY, and a third MOTIVE.

"What is this, the FBI at work or what?" cracked Zach.

"Quiet," said Rachel. "If we're going to solve this mystery, we're going to do it the way real detectives do. Every reasonable suspect has to have two things: the opportunity to commit the crime and a motive or reason for doing it."

"And Sue has both," said Andy. "As a member of the team she would've had plenty of opportunity to learn what the old signs were. And, like we just said, she could have picked up the new signs by spying on us at our prepractice session the other day."

"Her motive is just as clear," offered Seth. "Revenge on the Sluggers for not getting the infield position she really wanted."

Rachel filled in the information on her suspect chart.

"Okay," said Rachel, wiping chalk off her freckled nose, "are there any other suspects?"

"The man with the camera in the stands!" exclaimed Zach. "The one with the zoom lens."

"Sure! With that zoom lens of his, and from where he was sitting, he had a perfect view of Andy's signals," said Rachel.

"And according to Marty, he was also at the Mudshark game and took pictures there, too," pointed out Seth.

"Who is this man?" asked Andy. "Does anyone recognize him?"

"Maybe he's a Major League scout who's come to the town of Lotus Pines to find a star pitcher," kidded Zach.

"Yeah, right!" answered Rachel. "This cameraman is no scout, and he's nobody I've ever seen before. He's certainly nobody's father on our team."

"Maybe he's related to one of the Tigers," said Seth excitedly. "If so, that would give him a motive for stealing the signs. To help his kid's team win the game."

Andy frowned. "You really think a parent would pull a dirty trick like that just so his kid could win a ball game?"

The others thought about this for a moment. Then Zach spoke up.

"Look, Andy," he said. "Some parents do get carried away with their kids' baseball games. Isn't it just possible that some father would go a bit too far to help his kid win?"

"It's possible," said Andy quietly, "but I hate to think it's true."

Rachel nodded silently but began to add this second suspect to the chalkboard.

"One thing we're all forgetting," spoke up Seth. "This guy was taking pictures *during* the game. Yet the Tigers were playing as if they already had the new signs. How could he have gotten the film developed and showed it to the Tigers while the game was still being played?"

"No sweat," said Rachel. "He saw Andy signaling

through his zoom, passed the info on early in the game, then took the pictures to share with the Tigers later. This way they'd remember the signs for the future."

"And maybe to share with the other teams," added Andy.

A light bulb went on in Zach's head. "That would explain it," he muttered.

"Explain what?" asked Seth.

"Explain why I was able to strike out the first two batters in the game," said Zach. "They didn't have the signs yet. Old Zoomie only figured them out in time to pass them on to the third batter, who got a hit off me."

"It all makes sense," said Rachel. "That would explain the Tigers' surprise time-out in the first inning. The one with all the whispering and pointing—and no coach. They must have been passing on the signs the camera guy stole."

"Good! But let's not get too far ahead of ourselves," said Seth. "At least not yet. Any more suspects?"

"I think I have one," said Andy. Then he told his friends about the girl with the floppy red hat and the binoculars—the one he had seen in the stands.

"Anyone recognize this girl from Andy's description?" asked Rachel.

"Nope, didn't notice any suspicious red hats," cracked Zach. "Or dangerous-looking binoculars."

"Wait a minute," said Rachel. "A good pair of binoculars is as handy for seeing signals as a zoom lens is. And the girl could have passed on the information to the Tigers just as easily as old Zoomie. We've got another suspect."

The four reviewed the chart Rachel had written neatly on the chalkboard.

Suspect	Opportunity	Motive
1. Susan Stein	Spying on teammates	Revenge on team
2. Man with Camera	Snapping pictures of signals	Help son's team to win game (?)
3. Girl with Binoculars	Seeing signals from stands	Help Tigers win (?)

"So what next?" asked Andy.

"We divide our forces and track our suspects," replied Rachel. "Andy, you're the only one who saw the girl and knows what she looks like. You go after her. Find out who she is and try to talk to her if you can. We've got to find out if she has a motive to steal the signals."

"I'm on the case," grinned Andy.

"Seth, your assignment is Zoomie," continued Rachel. "learn who he is and if he's got a son or daughter on either the Tigers or the Mudsharks. If so, then we can go after his kid and learn the truth about that camera."

"Leave it to me," said Seth confidently.

"So I get to watch Sue Stein?" said Zach disappointedly. "That doesn't sound like much fun."

"You got it all wrong," said Rachel. "I get Sue. She's

my friend and I think I can draw her out better than anyone else. *You* get to practice your pitching."

"What?" yelled Zach. "You mean you three are going to be running around detecting while I play ball? That's not fair!"

"Your job is to stay in shape for our upcoming game against the Rocket Raiders next Saturday," continued Rachel. "We don't need you worrying about this mystery when you're out on the mound."

"If everyone in the world, including the Raiders, knows our signals, it's not going to make much difference how well I pitch," complained Zach. "Unless you guys think we should talk to the coach about changing the signs again."

"No," said Rachel. "I think it's important we keep them the same for the next game. It just might help lead us to the sign stealer."

"With any luck, we might know who it is by then," said Seth.

"Optimist," said Rachel.

Before Zach could open his mouth, Rachel grabbed the dictionary from under the television and handed it to him.

"Look it up!" she smiled.

5 A Puzzling Interview

It was Monday lunchtime in the school cafeteria and Andy was looking for a place to sit when his friend Sam waved to him from an empty table. Sam had already finished eating and Andy could tell, from the greedy way he eyed his french fries, that Sam was as happy to see Andy's lunch as he was to see Andy.

"Hi, Sam," he said as he sat down. "What did you think of the game on Saturday?" Andy knew Sam's love of food was only surpassed by his love of baseball. He never missed a league game.

"You guys got massacred," Sam said flatly. "But you played well," he quickly added. "The Tigers just played better."

"Thanks," said Andy. "Care for a french fry?"

"Sure you don't mind?"

Before Andy could say he didn't mind at all, Sam had already stuffed two greasy fries into his waiting mouth.

"By the way," said Andy casually, as he watched Sam eat his fries, "did you notice that girl with the floppy red hat in the stands at the game? The one with the binoculars?"

"That's Jennifer Barinski," mumbled Sam through a mouthful of fries. "She comes to all her brother's games."

"Who's her brother?" asked Andy, hoping he wasn't sounding too eager.

"Jeff Barinski, of course. He plays first base for the Tigers."

"No kidding?" replied Andy. "That's great."

Sam stopped eating to look curiously at his friend. "What's so great about it?" he said. "Jeff hit a home run in the fifth inning against you guys."

"He sure did," said Andy softly. "And now I think I know how he did it."

"What?" asked Sam, wiping salt from his fingers with a paper napkin.

"Nothing," replied Andy. "I was just talking to myself."

He looked down to see one lonely french fry left in the middle of his plate.

"Sorry about that," said Sam, who couldn't take his eyes off that last fry. "I didn't mean to eat them all."

"It's okay," smiled Andy. "I wasn't that hungry anyway. You go ahead and finish it."

"Gee, thanks!" exclaimed Sam, popping the fry into his mouth. "You're a real pal, Andy."

"So are you," replied the catcher. "Say, Sam, you wouldn't happen to know what class Jennifer Barinski's in? I have a message I want to give her for her brother."

Seth Bradigan had also done some detective work during lunchtime. He had gone to Photo Supreme. It was the only shop in town that carried those big zoom lenses. Seth described the man with the camera to the owner. The owner said that it sounded just like Arthur Woods of the Woods Real Estate Agency. In fact, Mr. Woods had recently bought an expensive zoom lens.

Seth rushed home from school, grabbed a snack, and looked up the agency's address in the phone book. After running an errand for his mother, Seth headed directly for Mr. Woods' office.

The Woods Agency was located on the second floor of a new, shiny office building on Main Street. As he walked up the stairs, Seth reviewed once more in his mind what he was going to say. He didn't want to slip up.

A woman wearing glasses sat behind a big desk in the reception area. She was about Seth's mother's age and smiled when he walked into the office.

"May I help you, young man?" she said pleasantly.

"Is Mr. Woods in?" Seth asked politely.

"No, but he should be back any minute," she told him. "Is there something I can help you with?"

"Well, I play in the Lotus Pines Youth Baseball League," began Seth, "and we're collecting donations for new baseball equipment. I thought Mr. Woods might like to make a contribution."

"Why, isn't that a coincidence," said the woman. "Mr. Woods' son Dave plays in that league, too. His team is the Toyshop Tigers. What team do you play for?"

"The Southside Sluggers," said Seth, trying not to react openly to the information he had just received.

"Dave's team won their first game of the season on Saturday," continued the woman, who obviously enjoyed talking. "I think Mr. Woods is more excited about it than Dave himself."

"Fathers are like that," Seth replied. *But not too many fathers would help their sons win by cheating,* he thought silently.

"Of course, Dave's not the only ball player in the family," said the woman.

"Oh?"

"There's his younger brother, Phil," she went on. "He plays on a league team, too."

"Which team?" asked Seth, trying to sound as casual as possible.

The woman adjusted her glasses and concentrated. "Let's see now," she said. "It's a funny name. Dirt something, I think . . . no, not dirt . . . Oh, what is it?"

"It doesn't happen to start with *Mud*, does it?" said Seth, helpfully.

"That's it, *Mud!*" exclaimed the woman. "The Mudfish, or something like that."

"Mudsharks!"

"That's it. Mudsharks! You know the team?"

"Oh, I know them all right," said Seth.

"Well, now," said the woman. "What was it exactly you wanted to see Mr. Woods about again?"

"Oh, nothing really," said Seth. "I'm collecting donations, but since he has two sons who play, he probably already has —"

Just then the door opened and the man with the camera from the ball game entered the office. He was wearing a business suit—just like on the day of the game. And he looked as if he was in a hurry.

"Oh, Mr. Woods," said the woman. "This young man wanted to speak to you."

Mr. Woods turned suddenly to Seth and smiled. "Oh?" he said.

"He plays on Dave's ball team," she told him.

"Really?" said Mr. Woods. "Well, you'd better come into my office, son."

Seth figured he'd gotten enough information for one visit but could see no way to leave gracefully. He took a deep breath and followed Mr. Woods into the office at the rear of the reception area.

The businessman sat down at his desk and motioned to a chair on the other side. Seth sat down and tried to decide what his next move would be.

"Now," said Mr. Woods breezily, "what position

do you play on the Tigers? I don't think I recall seeing you before."

Seth swallowed. "Actually, sir, I don't play for the Tigers," he explained. "The woman outside got it a little mixed up. I'm the left fielder for the Sluggers. My name is Seth Bradigan."

"Oh?" said Mr. Woods, leaning back in his chair. "Aren't you the team the Tigers beat on Saturday?"

"They beat us, all right," said Seth.

Just then the phone rang sharply on Mr. Woods' desk. He asked Seth to excuse him, picked up the receiver, and began talking earnestly to the person on the other end.

Seth wanted nothing better than to tiptoe quietly out of the office and head for home. But that was impossible. Anyway, there was more information to be gotten here. If only he knew how to get it.

He suddenly wished he had asked Rachel to come along with him. He felt she would do a far better job of finding out if Mr. Woods was responsible for the stolen signs.

Just then, Seth noticed a camera and some rolls of film on top of a file cabinet. Next to the camera was a new zoom lens—just like the one he had seen Mr. Woods using at Saturday's game.

Mr. Woods finished talking and hung up the phone.

"Sorry about the interruption," he said. "Now what was it you wanted to see me about, Seth?"

"I was going to ask for a donation for new equipment for our team," said Seth. "But since your sons both play, I guess you've already given money to their teams."

"That's true," admitted Mr. Woods. "But I suppose I could make a small donation. I always like to help out you ball players. Baseball's a great sport for young people. It builds character. I used to play myself when I was your age. I played ball in high school, too. I was a star pitcher in my day."

"Really?" said Seth.

Mr. Woods grabbed a pen on his desk and wrote something quickly. Then he handed a surprised Seth a check for twenty-five dollars.

"I, uh, can't take this," said Seth, staring at the check.

Mr. Woods looked curiously at him. "Why not?" he asked. "You need the money. I know how expensive equipment can be. I've bought enough bats and gloves for those two boys of mine, believe me."

Seth could have kicked himself for nearly blowing his cover story. He thanked Mr. Woods and got up. He couldn't help looking once more at the camera. "Do you take lots of pictures?" he asked.

"All the time," replied Mr. Woods. "Photography is my main hobby, you might say. My family is always teasing, saying that I take pictures of everything. In fact, I just got this fabulous zoom lens."

"Do you ever take pictures of . . . ball games?" Seth asked.

There was an abrupt pause in the conversation. The friendly smile was still on Mr. Woods' face, but his eyes narrowed on Seth. "Why do you ask?" he said.

"No reason," said Seth. "I just remembered seeing someone at the game on Saturday with a zoom lens and a camera just like that one. I thought it might have been you."

"I think you've mistaken me for someone else," said Mr. Woods quickly. "I was at the game, but I didn't take any pictures."

Seth was about to say something else but the man cut him short.

"It was nice to meet you, Seth," he said, ushering the boy out his door. "Good luck with your fund-raising. Mrs. Holden, will you show this young man out?"

The office door shut quickly and Seth stared in bewilderment at the woman behind the reception desk.

"How did it go?" she asked him.

Seth held out the check for her to see.

"Mr. Woods is such a generous man," she said. "I knew he'd give you what you wanted."

Seth had to disagree. He had gotten more than he had bargained for.

6 What's Wrong with the Center Fielder?

The Rocket Raiders were one ball team that didn't need to cheat to win. They had been league champions for two seasons and had won every game they had played so far this season. When they met the Sluggers in Bloom Field that Saturday afternoon, the Sluggers had little reason to be hopeful.

However, Seth, Rachel, Andy, and Zach were ready to give them a good fight. The idea that the Raiders might have been given their signals by the Mudsharks or Tigers made the four Sluggers angry. They were determined to win in spite of everything.

Zach and Andy decided before the game not to use any signals at all. For a while, this strategy seemed to work. Zach's pitching was sharp early on and he struck out a couple of batters. In fact, the Raiders' only run in the first two innings was off a bunt single and two errors by shortstop Ernie Peters.

But Zach soon realized just how much he relied on Andy's knowledge of each batter. Andy's signals helped Zach key his pitches to a hitter's weakness. And, of course, tried to prevent him from throwing to a batter's strength.

Rob Spencer, captain of the Raiders and a heavy hitter, came up to bat in the third inning. Zach purposely threw him low inside pitches to avoid the long ball. But he forgot that Rob got most of his power from his strange golf-like swing. The Raider captain lifted one of Zach's low pitches over the center-field fence.

Rob's long golf shot shook Zach's confidence. Biff Morgan, another big hitter for the Raiders stalked up to the plate. Zach couldn't remember which pitch Biff had a hard time hitting. *Was it an inside fastball or a change-up?* Zach asked himself. He decided to go with the change-up.

The ball cracked against Biff's bat and went soaring into center field, right over Susan Stein's head. "Wrong pitch," Zach muttered to himself as Biff cruised into third base. The game was slipping away.

"I think you'd better start giving me signals again," Zach told Andy when the inning was over. "If we're going to lose, at least I want to lose pitching my best."

The Raiders were now ahead 6–1.

"I guess you're right," sighed Andy as they headed for the bench and waited for their turn at bat. "But I don't see why the Raiders need our signals to beat us.

They can do it just on their great playing."

Seth joined them on the bench. "Maybe nobody gave them our signals," he said. "Do you notice who's missing from the grandstands?"

Zach and Andy immediately looked up at where the spectators sat. The man with the camera was nowhere to be seen.

"It makes sense he isn't here," said Zach. "I mean, neither of his sons' teams is playing us today. He has no reason to help the Raiders beat us, right?"

Seth nodded in agreement. He had given his three friends a full report of his meeting with Mr. Woods at the office several days earlier.

"Of course," said Seth, "it could also mean that I scared him off when I said I'd seen him taking pictures at our game against the Tigers. Maybe that was a mistake. Now we may never know if he was the signal stealer or not."

"Don't get down on yourself," said Andy. "You did a great job. If you scared him off, good. Although, if you look closely, you'll see another suspect who *is* here."

Zach and Seth scanned the stands. The girl with the floppy hat was in the first row, peering intently through a large pair of black binoculars. This time she wore a blue hat, instead of a red one.

"Different hat, same binoculars," grinned Zach.

"I didn't believe it before," said Andy under his breath.

"Believe what?" asked Seth.

"The first time, I thought it was just my imagination, but now I know it's not," Andy said. "She's looking right at us."

It was true. As the Rocket Raiders' pitcher warmed up on the mound, the girl's binoculars were trained on the three Sluggers on the bench.

"I think I'll have a talk with old Floppy Hat after the game and find out just what she's looking at," said Andy.

"Good idea," said Zach. "Just remember to play it cool and don't give yourself away."

"You concentrate on your pitching," said Seth, playfully pulling Zach's cap down over his eyes. "Leave the detective work to us."

Meanwhile, a few yards away, Rachel sat down on the grass alongside Susan Stein.

"Too bad about that high fly," she said.

Susan gave her a quick look and then turned away. "Lay off, Rach," she said.

"Hey, it's okay," said Rachel, drawing closer. "It could've happened to anyone. The ball went right over your head. There was no way you could've laid a glove on it."

"Save the pep talk," said Susan, pulling at a blade of grass. "I could've caught it if I had thought ahead and gotten behind the ball. You know that as well as I do."

"Okay, maybe you could have," replied Rachel. "It's not the end of the world."

Rachel looked directly at Susan. "What's going on?"

Rachel said. "We used to be friends. I can't seem to talk to you lately."

Susan shifted her eyes away from Rachel. "I don't know what you're talking about," she said.

Rachel took a deep breath and continued. "Look, Susan," she said, "if something's bothering you—anything at all—you can tell me. I'm your friend."

Susan got up and brushed the dirt from her uniform. "The only thing that's bothering me right now is *you*. Why can't you just leave me alone?"

Before Rachel could reply, Susan walked off to the batter's box. Rachel watched her go. *Is my brother right?* she wondered. *Is Susan's conscience bothering her? And if so, for what reason?* Rachel didn't like to think about the answers she came up with.

By the fifth inning, the Raiders seemed to be hitting everything Andy called for. They were waiting on the change-ups and timing the fastballs. Zach seemed ready to just throw up his hands and quit.

The final score was a predictable Raiders 13, Sluggers 4. Poor Zach walked off the field in a daze. He had pitched the whole game. But he couldn't figure out if it was the stolen signals, his pitching, or the Raiders' great playing that had defeated his team.

"Maybe it was a combination of all three things," suggested Seth as they headed out of the park. "Although I can't see why the Raiders would need to cheat to win."

"Maybe knowing our signals was just insurance," said Andy.

Zach shook his head in bewilderment. "I don't know," he admitted. "This whole signal-stealing mystery keeps getting more and more confusing."

Andy's attention suddenly shifted as he saw Jennifer Barinski's floppy blue hat in the crowd of kids leaving the park ahead of them.

"Excuse me, guys," he said. "I've got to catch up with my suspect. Maybe she has the answer to our mystery — her and her binoculars."

"Good luck," said Seth.

Andy ran ahead. He found Jennifer chatting with a group of girls in the parking lot. A big cast covered her right leg from the foot to just below the knee.

"What happened to your foot?" Andy asked.

"I guess I got my roller skates a little crossed," the girl said, turning around. Under the floppy hat was a tanned face with big blue eyes that matched her hat.

"Sorry about that! I'm Andy," he said a little shyly. "Andy West. It rhymes with 'best.' "

"Hi, I'm Jennifer Barinski," she laughed. "I don't see how you can say that you're the 'best' after losing a game."

"It's our third loss in a row," answered Andy with good humor. "We're getting used to it. You must like to watch us lose."

"Why do you say that?" asked Jennifer.

"I've noticed you at our last two games," explained

Andy. "And since your brother's team wasn't playing against us this time, I thought—"

"Jennifer!" called a girl from the front seat of a car in the parking lot. Jennifer turned her head and waved.

"That's my friend. Her mom is giving me a ride home," she said to Andy. "I'm afraid I have to go. It was nice meeting you, Andy. I hope you guys do better the next time you play."

"Wait a sec," cried Andy, as Jennifer started to leave. "I was wondering if maybe we could talk again."

"Sure," said Jennifer. "When?"

"How about after school on Monday at the Southside Ice Cream Shop?"

Jennifer thought for a moment and then smiled. "That sounds fine. I'll meet you there Monday right after school."

"See you then!" called Andy.

Andy wondered why such a nice girl would help her brother's team cheat. And if she did, why would she be so friendly with him—the catcher for the Sluggers.

All Rachel could think about after the game was her talk with Susan. That bothered her even more than losing to the Raiders. She was so busy thinking about Susan that she forgot her fielder's glove at the ballpark. She was halfway home before she realized she'd left it behind.

By the time Rachel got back to Bloom Field, the place was deserted. She found her glove where she'd

left it, under the bench. She was starting to leave, when she heard two voices coming from under the grandstand.

Rachel walked over to the grandstand and saw two people, both in Youth Baseball League uniforms, standing in the shadows under the stands. One player, a girl, had her back to Rachel. The other one she recognized as Rob Spencer, captain of the Rocket Raiders.

"You've got to make up your mind about this," Rob was saying. "It's them or us."

"You have to give me more time," the other player said. "I need time to think it over."

Rachel recognized the voice right away. It was Susan Stein's.

"I don't know why," said Rob. "After the way they've treated you, it's what they deserve."

Susan turned away. "Yeah, I know," was all she said. "Just give me some time."

"Okay," Rob said at last. "I'll give you a week to make up your mind. After that, we'll have to go with someone else. It's up to you."

"I'll let you know," sighed Susan, and she started to walk away.

Rachel dropped to the ground to avoid being seen as the two came out from under the stands. She looked up just in time to catch a glimpse of her friend's face. Susan looked very upset.

7 Jennifer's Confession

Andy arrived early at the ice-cream shop on Monday afternoon. He sat at a booth waiting for Jennifer. Mr. Langlin, the owner, came over. Mr. Langlin was tall and thin like Zach, but he had Rachel's bright red hair.

"All alone, Andy?" he asked. "Where's the gang?" Mr. Langlin was used to seeing the Sluggers come into his shop as a group.

"I don't know, Mr. Langlin," Andy said. "I'm waiting for someone—a new friend."

"Well, while you're waiting, maybe you'd like to try a dish of my newest flavor of ice cream."

The shop owner leaned over on the table. "Caramel Carrot Crunch," he whispered in Andy's ear.

"That sounds . . . great," said Andy.

It really didn't, but he knew how Mr. Langlin prided

himself on his new flavors. He created each one himself in the back of the ice-cream shop. Some of his flavors, like Orang-u-tang Chip, were popular with his customers. Others, like Pickleberry Sundae, were marketing disasters.

But this didn't bother Mr. Langlin. He faithfully kept each flavor in stock, no matter how poorly it sold. Andy had a sneaking feeling that Caramel Carrot Crunch would be about as popular as Pickleberry Sundae.

"Well, what do you say, Andy?" persisted Mr. Langlin. "Since you're a preferred customer, the first dish of Caramel Carrot Crunch is on the house."

Andy's stomach was feeling a little jittery over his upcoming meeting with Jennifer. He didn't think Mr. Langlin's latest flavor would improve it. "Maybe a little later, Mr. Langlin," he said. "After my friend gets here."

"Sure," said the owner. Then he disappeared behind the counter.

A moment later the front door swung open and Jennifer hobbled in on her cast. She was wearing a yellow floppy hat this time.

"Sorry I'm late," she apologized. "It takes me longer to get around these days."

"I see," said Andy. "By the way, I like your new hat!"

Before Jennifer could look at the menu, Mr. Langlin reappeared like a shot.

"Hello," he said warmly. "How about a double scoop of Caramel Carrot Crunch ice cream? It's today's special."

"Caramel Carrot Crunch?" Jennifer repeated. "I never heard of *that* flavor before!"

Mr. Langlin smiled with all the pride of a creative genius. "Of course you haven't heard of it before," he explained. "I invented it myself. It's the twelfth new flavor sold exclusively at the Southside Ice Cream Shop and nowhere else."

Jennifer looked impressed, but still uncertain. "That's great, but I don't know about—"

"Your first dish is completely free," Mr. Langlin added quickly. "No charge!"

"Well, all right," said Jennifer.

"Two Caramel Carrot Crunches, coming up!" cried Mr. Langlin, heading for the counter.

Jennifer looked at Andy. "Is he always so . . . excited about his flavors?" she asked.

"Only when he's just invented a new one," grinned Andy. "He gets all worked up, like a mad scientist in a laboratory."

Jennifer laughed. Andy laughed, too. The giggling almost made Andy forget why he had asked Jennifer to meet him.

"I'm really glad we're having this talk, Andy," said Jennifer. "You see, I have a confession to make."

"Oh?" said Andy.

"I didn't come to your game against the Tigers to see my brother play," she said.

"You didn't?"

"No, I came to . . ." Jennifer paused, embarrassed. "Well, I have a feeling you already know what I'm about to say. I mean, you saw me at the game with my binoculars, didn't you?"

So she's the sign stealer, after all, Andy thought. *Amazing!*

Jennifer's tanned face was beginning to redden. "It's not easy for me to talk about it."

Andy suddenly felt sorry for her. "That's okay," he said "I'm sure you wouldn't have done it on your own. Your brother put you up to it, didn't he?"

Jennifer looked surprised. "My *brother*?" she gasped. "Are you kidding? If he knew, he'd probably brain me. He thinks *he's* the greatest player in the league."

Now it was Andy's turn to look confused. "But I don't understand—"

Before he could finish his sentence, Mr. Langlin appeared with two generous dishes of an orange-and-white-colored ice cream.

"Here we go," he said, placing the dishes in front of Andy and Jennifer. "Enjoy!"

Jennifer carefully examined the ice cream. "What are those orange things in it?" she asked Mr. Langlin.

"That's the carrot," explained the ice cream inventor. "That's what gives it the crunch."

"Oh," said Jennifer. She continued to stare at the dish.

Mr. Langlin was hoping to see Jennifer's reaction to her first bite, but when he saw her hold back he reluctantly returned to the counter.

As soon as he was out of earshot, Andy spoke again in a low voice.

"Jennifer, if your brother didn't ask you, why would you ever do such a thing?" he wanted to know.

"I don't know what you're talking about," she replied. "And why are you speaking so quietly?"

"I don't want Mr. Langlin to hear us," Andy replied. "He's the sponsor of our team. What would he think of you if he found out?"

"I don't see why it should concern him," said Jennifer. "The only person it concerns is your teammate, Seth Bradigan."

"What does Seth have to do with any of this?" Andy asked, bewildered.

"Everything!" replied Jennifer. "I usually play left field—when I'm not hurt. And Seth is the best left fielder I've seen this season."

Andy's chin nearly dropped into his two scoops of Caramel Carrot Crunch.

"You mean to say at every game you've been watching *Seth* through your binoculars?"

"Of course," Jennifer said. "It's impossible to see him clearly in the outfield without binoculars. He's really great. I can pick up a lot of good pointers for next season. I especially like the way he protects the left-field line."

"Yeah, he's great all right," said Andy, still a little surprised.

"I'd like to meet Seth," said Jennifer. "I have a lot of questions for him."

Just then, Mr. Langlin came back looking disappointed.

"Your ice cream's melting," he said to Andy.

Andy sighed, picked up his spoon and took a big bite from his dish.

"What do you think?" asked Mr. Langlin anxiously.

Andy swallowed hard and tried to smile.

"Delicious," he said.

8 Mr. Woods Throws a Curveball

It was not a happy group of Sluggers that met in Seth Bradigan's downstairs den Tuesday afternoon. Sure, it was good news that Jennifer Barinski was not the sign stealer. But Rachel's report about the conversation she'd overheard between Susan Stein and Raider captain Rob Spencer was upsetting.

The only Slugger who seemed in high spirits was Seth. "I never realized what a popular player I am," he said as he lay on the couch tossing a ball in the air. "I guess I can give Jennifer a few fielding pointers."

"Don't let your head swell too much, hotshot," replied Zach. "If we keep losing ball games, even Jennifer Barinski is going to lose interest in your playing."

Seth smiled. "You're just jealous because someone is more interested in my fielding than your pitching," he said.

"Someone is very interested in Zach's pitching," corrected Rachel. "Interested enough to steal our signs in order to know what those pitches are. It's cost us three games and now it's got to stop. Our next game against the Mudsharks is exactly one week away. We've got to catch the sign stealer before next Tuesday."

"Can't we just ask Coach Terwilliger to change the signs again?" asked Andy.

"What good will that do?" reasoned Seth. "Whoever stole our signs before can probably steal them again. The only way to stop it once and for all is to find out who it is—and how they're getting the signs."

"Seth's right," said Zach. "We can't afford to lose another game. Especially not to those miserable Mudsharks. We'll be the joke of the entire league!"

Rachel crossed Jennifer's name off the list of suspects on the chalkboard.

"It looks as if Susan has become our prime suspect," Rachel said. "I still can't forget that conversation I overheard after the game. 'It's them or us,' Rob Spencer said to Susan. 'Us' being the Raiders and 'them' being our team. What doesn't make sense to me is why Rob would have to ask her for the signs if Susan had already given them to the Mudsharks and the Tigers."

"Maybe she made a separate deal with each team to sell the signs," suggested Zach. "The Raiders were just the last one on her list."

"You're way off base," replied Rachel. "Susan's not that kind of person. I can't believe she'd give the signs away for any reason—even if she was still angry about not getting the position she wanted."

Seth pounded the baseball into his fielder's glove. "If that's so, then why would Susan put the Raiders off about giving them the signs? It's a little late for her conscience to start bothering her, isn't it?"

Nobody spoke for a moment. Then Rachel said, "Maybe she's having second thoughts."

"Maybe," said Andy thoughtfully. "But what do you make of the last thing Rob said to Susan? 'I'll give you a week to make up your mind. After that, we'll have to go with someone else.' Who could 'someone else' possibly be?"

"It couldn't be another member of our team, could it?" asked Zach.

"It's possible," said Seth. "It's like when countries recruit spies from another country. They look for someone who's dissatisfied or has a grudge. They go after that person to spy for them. If they could find Susan, maybe they figure they could find someone else who would do the same thing."

No one liked to think another team member would be giving away their secrets. The discussion ended for a while. Then Rachel got up and circled Mr. Woods on the suspect list.

"We still can't discount Mr. Woods," she told her friends. "He has as much a motive as Susan does—at least for the games his sons played in. Through that zoom lens on his camera, he could easily have seen our signs."

"But how are we going to prove he did it?" argued Seth. "After my first meeting with him, he'll be on his guard. He'll never give himself away. And remember, Mr. Woods wasn't at the Raiders' game."

The four friends pondered this problem. Rachel scratched her red hair as she concentrated. Zach, deep in thought, unconsciously stuck out his tongue. Seth pounded the baseball into his mitt. Andy just sat there staring up at the ceiling.

"Put your tongue back in your mouth, Zach," scolded Rachel. "It makes you look silly."

Zach was sensitive about his tongue. He just couldn't break his habit of sticking it out.

"I'll stick in my tongue when you stop scratching your hair," he snapped back. Rachel quickly dropped the subject.

"Wait a minute," said Andy at last. "I talked to Jennifer and found out what she was really doing at the ballpark. We should be able to do the same by just talking with Mr. Woods."

Seth stopped popping the ball into his mitt. "Right!" he said jokingly. "I'm going to walk back into his office and ask him if he stole our signs so his sons' teams could beat us. You think if he's guilty he's going to say yes?"

"No," said Rachel. "But not many people I know can tell a lie without giving themselves away. Especially if you catch them off their guard. I think we'll know whether or not Mr. Woods is telling the truth."

"So what if he lies and we know he's guilty," worried Zach. "How is that going to stop the sign stealing?"

"If he knows we know, it just might be enough to scare him off," replied Andy. "I think it's worth a try."

"Anyway, Seth, you have the perfect excuse to go back to his office," pointed out Rachel. "I mean, you haven't returned that check Mr. Woods gave you."

Seth looked embarrassed. He had meant to return the check days ago but had put it off.

"To tell you the truth, I'd rather deal with Susan Stein than Mr. Woods," Seth confessed. "It was hard enough for me to walk into his office the first time. This time it'll be ten times worse."

"You're not getting cold feet, are you?" kidded Zach.

"No, Seth's right," said Rachel. "This is one visit he shouldn't have to handle alone. We're all going down to see Mr. Woods."

"When?" asked Andy.

"Right now."

Mrs. Holden, Mr. Woods' receptionist, was sitting at the front desk just as she had been the last time Seth visited the agency. Rachel, Andy, and Zach stood beside their friend as he asked the woman if Mr. Woods was in.

"Why yes," she replied, peering at him through her

glasses. "Aren't you the boy who was here a while ago asking for money for your baseball team?"

"That's right," said Seth uneasily.

"Well, I'll go see if he's free," she said and went into the inner office.

The four friends waited anxiously. In Seth's den, it had seemed a good idea to confront Mr. Woods. But now that they were standing in his office, it was a different matter. Even Rachel had lost some of her confidence.

Mrs. Holden returned, smiling. "Mr. Woods will see you now."

Seth led the way into the office.

Arthur Woods was sitting at his desk in his shirtsleeves. He looked up from some papers on his desk when the quartet entered. Seeing Seth, he smiled. But there was an uneasiness in the smile that didn't escape Rachel's eye. *He looks guilty,* she thought.

"Well, hello," he said heartily to Seth. "I see you brought your whole team with you this time. Or at least half of it."

Seth introduced the businessman to his three friends.

"I hope this visit is for pleasure and not business, like the last one," chuckled Mr. Woods.

"You might say it *is* business," answered Rachel. "Seth wanted to return the check you gave him."

The man looked surprised. "I don't understand," he said.

Seth spoke up, before Rachel could speak for him.

"You see, sir," he began, "I really didn't come here last time to collect money. That was just an excuse to get in to see you."

Mr. Woods' eyes narrowed and the smile disappeared. "What is this all about?" he asked.

"It's about your picture-taking at our ball games, Mr. Woods," said Seth.

"What about it?" asked the man. "I take pictures of everything. Photography is my hobby."

"Maybe so," spoke up Zach. "But these pictures of our games concern us." He paused to take a deep breath. "You see, someone has been stealing our pitching signals and we can't figure out how they're doing it unless someone is helping them."

Mr. Woods' face went blank. Then he rubbed his chin and looked at them. "You think that I've been taking pictures of your pitching signals and giving them to other teams?" he said, with an amazed look on his face.

None of the Sluggers spoke for a tense moment. Then Rachel broke the silence. "No disrespect, Mr. Woods," she said. "But when Seth found out that your sons play for the Mudsharks and the Toyshop Tigers, we couldn't help being suspicious."

Mr. Woods continued rubbing his chin. "I'm beginning to understand now," he said slowly. "Both those teams beat you when I was there watching, didn't they?"

All four nodded.

"Before you say anything more," said Mr. Woods, "I think I'd better show you something."

He got up from his chair and went over to a small closet. He opened the door and took out several large, blown-up pictures matted on thick cardboard. One picture was of Phil Woods in his Mudshark uniform catching a fly ball. Another showed Dave Woods, bat in hand, hitting the ball for the Toyshop Tigers.

"They're great pictures," said Andy.

"And the only way I could take them from the stands was with my zoom lens," explained Mr. Woods. "When you thought I was taking pictures of your signals, I was actually shooting my two sons playing. You see, Phil's birthday is this month. And Dave's is in July. I wanted to take pictures of them playing in a game and then give the pictures to them as birthday presents. Only I wanted to do it secretly, so it would be a surprise."

"Which explains why you didn't want to talk to me when I brought up the subject of your picture-taking last time," said Seth.

"Exactly," said Mr. Woods with a sheepish grin. "Since you were in the league I was afraid you might say something to your teammates and word would get back to Dave and Phil. That would spoil the surprise."

"Talk about a misunderstanding!" exclaimed Rachel. "We're really sorry we ever thought that you—"

"Don't mention it," interrupted Mr. Woods.

"Everybody makes mistakes. If I were in your shoes I'd probably come to the same conclusion. Are you sure about the sign stealing?"

"About as sure as we can be," said Zach. "Every game the batters know my pitches before the ball leaves my glove."

Mr. Woods looked concerned. "These things do happen," he said with a sigh. "I remember teams stealing signs when I played ball in college. It made me and my teammates awfully angry when we found out. I wish there was something I could do to help. I'll talk to my sons about it. Maybe they can ask around."

"Thanks," said Rachel, but with little enthusiasm in her voice. Like her three friends, she knew they had narrowed their suspects down to one person. And they didn't need the help of the Woods boys to figure out who the guilty party was.

Seth took a piece of folded paper from his pocket. "Oh, before I forget, here's your check back, sir," he said.

Mr. Woods took one look at the twenty-five-dollar check in Seth's hand and shook his head. "You keep it," he said. "Give it to your coach. He'll know how to best spend it for your team."

"But we couldn't," protested Rachel.

"Consider it repayment for the trouble I unintentionally caused you."

"Boy, we sure had him figured wrong, didn't we?" said Seth, as they stepped back out into the street.

"Yeah," said Zach. "This leaves us with just one suspect—Susan."

"Maybe we should all talk to her," suggested Andy. "Just like we did with Mr. Woods."

Rachel shook her head. "No," she said quietly but firmly. "This is something I have to do by myself."

9 Big Game, Big Trouble

Coach Terwilliger arrived early at Bloom Field on the following Tuesday for the game between the Mudsharks and the Sluggers. The coach was worried. For three weeks his team had been in a slump—losing three games in a row.

Now the Sluggers were going up against the lowly Mudsharks again. If they lost this game, the whole team might just give up. The coach wanted to do everything possible to get his players ready to win.

The rumors about sign stealing also bothered the Coach. He had done a little investigating on his own and could find no evidence of stealing. That, however, didn't mean it wasn't going on.

Coach Terwilliger could see that at least four of his key players believed in the sign stealing and that it was having a negative effect on their playing. While changing the signs again might help, the coach decided it would be better to just give his players a few tips and a pep talk before the game.

One by one the players arrived on the field. Rachel and Zach came together. Rachel was looking anxiously for Susan, who was nowhere to be seen.

Rachel had spent a good part of the weekend and Monday evening trying to reach her friend. But every time she called, Mrs. Stein said Susan was either out or unable to come to the phone. On Monday, she wasn't even in school. With the game about to start, Rachel was beside herself.

Then all at once, Susan came trotting across the field toward the dugout.

"Susan, we have to talk," Rachel said urgently. She led her friend behind the dugout where they wouldn't be disturbed.

Susan didn't look any more willing to talk with Rachel than she had during the Raiders' game. But she didn't resist.

"Why didn't you return my calls?" Rachel demanded.

"I didn't feel like talking to you," Susan replied. "Can't this wait? It's almost time for the game to start."

"It can't wait," said Rachel abruptly. "What's the matter with you, Susan? You've got to tell me what's going on with you. If you're angry at your teammates, why don't you just quit the team?"

Susan looked at her friend in complete astonishment. "How did you know about that?" she said.

"I overheard you talking to Rob Spencer after our last game," replied Rachel.

"Then . . . you know?"

The talking and laughter of the fans in the grandstand grew louder, but Rachel hardly heard it. "Susan," she said softly. "How could you do it? How could you betray your own team?"

"I haven't!" exclaimed Susan. "Oh, I thought about it. Sure. But then I realized just how much the Sluggers mean to me—despite how I felt when I didn't get third base. So the very next day I called Rob and told him to find somebody else to play third for the Raiders. I wasn't interested."

"Play for the Raiders?" asked Rachel, totally confused.

"Rob Spencer has been after me for weeks to quit the Sluggers and join his team," explained Susan. "Their third-base player is moving away from Lotus Pines and they need a replacement fast. Rob offered me the position. It was a tough decision for me and I guess I felt pretty rotten trying to make up my mind. I'm sorry if I took it out on you, Rach."

Rachel could hardly believe her ears. "Then you mean that you didn't give our signals to the Mudsharks and the Tigers?" she asked.

"Of course not!" cried Susan. "Why would I ever do a dumb thing like that?"

Rachel felt happy and terrible at the same time. She was happy that her friend was not a traitor to the team. But she felt terrible because she had suspected her of being one.

Suddenly, Coach Terwilliger peeked his head around the corner of the dugout. "If you two are through chatting, I'd like to have a word with the team before we start this game," he said.

Susan and Rachel hustled into the dugout, where the other Sluggers were already gathered. The coach paced back and forth a bit before he began to speak.

"I know the Mudsharks beat us good the last time we played," he said. "And I'm no happier about that than you are. But we have a chance today to show them just how good we really are. Let's climb out of the cellar with a win—and put the Mudsharks back in last place.

A few players started to cheer, but the coach silenced them with a raised hand. "Zach's had some rough games lately," said the coach, looking at Zach and then at Robin Hayes. "But he's still our number-one pitcher. This is our only game this week—so I'm going to go with Zach as long as I can. Let's give it our best! Go out there and play ball!"

The team gave a shout and ran out onto the field. Zach and Seth rushed to Rachel's side.

"Did you talk to her?" they both wanted to know.

"Yes, and she's not the sign stealer," said Rachel.

"Are you sure?" Zach persisted.

"I'm sure."

"But if it's not Susan, then who *is* the sign stealer?" asked Seth, bewildered. "We've run out of suspects!"

"I don't know," admitted Rachel. "Maybe it doesn't matter anymore. Let's just get out there and play like the coach told us to. Give it your best, Zach!"

Zach nodded and strode out to the mound. He warmed up with Andy for a few minutes. Zach was relieved to hear about Susan, but at the same time he was more confused than ever. The only hope he could cling to now was that the Mudsharks might not know the new signals. After all, Coach Terwilliger had changed them after their last game against the Mudsharks.

Zach's pitching was strong, but not consistent. He was too caught up in worrying about the signs being stolen. He struck out the first batter and walked the next.

Chip Hoover, one of the Mudsharks' better hitters, let two fastballs go by before launching a change-up deep into left field. Seth, playing Chip deep, caught the ball on the run. A cheer went up in the stands.

Andy turned and smiled. There was Jennifer Barinski standing up with her binoculars, cheering loudly for her favorite outfielder.

The next batter anticipated an outside pitch and hit a line drive that shortstop Ernie Peters couldn't handle. That put runners on first and second with two outs. Zach was getting that terrible sinking feeling again. They seemed to have the signals.

Sure enough, the next Mudshark waited for a pitch down the middle and pounded it back to the center-field fence. Luckily, Susan dashed under it. She caught the ball with a great one-hand grab. The Sluggers escaped the top of the inning without giving up a run.

"Nice catch!" Rachel hollered to Susan as they headed for the infield.

"Thanks," said Susan. "I feel like a new ballplayer since I turned down the Raiders."

"I'm awfully glad you did," said Rachel sincerely. "We really need you, Sue."

Susan smiled warmly. It was the first time Rachel had seen her smile in a long time.

Rachel was the first batter up for the Sluggers. She hit a solid single up the middle. And then she alertly took off for second when the center fielder bobbled the ball.

Marty Franklin came up next. He tried twice to move Rachel to third with a sacrifice bunt. But each time he fouled the ball off. On the third pitch, he cracked a grounder to the second baseman. Marty was thrown out at first, but Rachel made it to third.

Seth came in determined to bring Rachel home. He took two mighty swings for two strikes. Then he surprised everybody with a bunt straight down the first-base line. He was tagged out easily, but there was no play on Rachel at home. The Sluggers led 1–0 at the end of the first inning. Rachel, Marty, and Seth had worked hard to manufacture a run.

By the end of the second inning. Zach was convinced that the Mudsharks knew the signals. They let Zach's fastballs and hard inside stuff go by. But the Mudsharks jumped on every fat change-up or pitch down the middle. They shifted in the batter's box as Zach went into his windup. Then they just waited for the pitch to come to them. Some great Slugger fielding limited the damage to only two runs in the second inning.

In the third inning, Zach picked up a grounder and threw to Marty Franklin at first. The ball sailed a foot over Marty's head. By the time Rachel retrieved the ball and hurled it to Luis at second, the Mudsharks were in scoring position.

Zach shifted his tongue to the other side of his mouth and pulled himself together. He managed to strike out the next batter with his best fastball. But two singles in a row—off two change-ups—gave the Mudsharks a 3–1 lead.

The bottom of the third produced a second run for the Sluggers. Susan Stein walked. Then Luis Diaz singled to left. Andy sent Susan home from second with a broken-bat single to right. Unfortunately, the rally ended on two strikeouts and a pop-up.

The Sluggers were down by only one run. But it seemed that the Mudsharks could explode at any time. After all, they had the Sluggers' number—and their signals.

Up at bat again in the fourth, the Mudsharks were getting cocky. No one more so than that one-time loser, Billy Butler. As Zach pitched, he could see the smug smile on Billy's face—and was determined to wipe it off. But Billy casually stepped into an outside change-up. The "Fly Swatter" was on first base with a clean single over second.

The next batter hit another solid single. That put runners on first and second with no outs.

Zach stepped off the mound. He was really upset. Andy couldn't tell if his friend was going to scream or cry.

The bottom was falling out for Zach. His face was covered with sweat, his energy was sinking, and his confidence in his pitching was at an all-time low.

From second base, Billy Butler couldn't resist adding insult to injury. He started to jeer loudly at Zach. "Come on, pitcher!" he shouted. "What's the matter with you? Have you got your signals crossed?"

When Zach heard this, his heart beat fast. He boiled over. The frustrations of the last three weeks hit him all at once. As Coach Terwilliger called for a brief time-out to confer with his pitcher, Zach ran over to second base.

"What was that you said about signals?" Zach asked Billy.

Billy pushed his glasses back on his nose and looked a bit startled. "Nothing," he said sullenly.

"You know our signs, don't you?" asked Seth, pulling the fuming Zach away from Billy. Rachel and Susan were moving in now from the outfield to hear what was being said.

Billy Butler looked around at the three outfielders

and the second-base player. He seemed to enjoy being the center of attention. And he got a special kick out of seeing Coach Terwilliger having to lead Zach away toward the pitcher's mound.

"Sure I know your signs," Billy bragged. "Everyone does."

Rachel advanced on the Mudshark. "Who gave them to you?" she demanded. "Who's the sign stealer?"

"Come on!" cried Susan. "Tell us! We have a right to know!"

"Okay, I'll tell you who it is," said Billy. "It's *him*." He pointed a finger at the pitcher's mound, where Zach now stood talking with Coach Terwilliger.

"The coach?" said Seth flabbergasted.

"No! *Zach Langlin!* He's the one!"

The four Sluggers stared incredulously at Zach. Before they could get another word out of Billy Butler, the umpire chased everyone back to their positions.

10 The Mystery Solved

"What's the matter with you guys?" Zach asked Seth and his sister as they came in from the outfield at mid-inning. "You two look like you just saw a ghost."

Rachel tried to avoid her brother's questioning eyes. "It's nothing, Zach," she managed to mumble.

Zach sighed. "Too bad," he said. "I was hoping maybe you had figured out who the sign stealer was."

Seth forced a grin. "No such luck," he said.

"Well, I guess I'd better practice a few swings," said the pitcher. "I'm up second at bat."

As soon as Zach had gone over to the on-deck circle, Seth pulled Rachel aside and spoke in a low whisper.

"Zach can't be the traitor," Seth said. "It's too ridiculous. Billy Butler's just trying to confuse us, that's all."

"I know," agreed Rachel. "And yet there was something that rang true about what he said."

"What are you two talking about?" asked Andy, coming over to them.

Seth filled the catcher in on what Billy Butler had said at second base.

"No way!" cried Andy. "Zach wouldn't do that. Butler is lying! They're the real stealers!"

"Maybe," said Rachel. "All the same, there was something about the way Billy talked that makes me wonder. I don't like him any more than you do. But when he said Zach was the stealer, it sounded as if he really meant it."

"Rach," protested Seth, "he *had* to be lying. Zach is your *brother*. You know he'd never deliberately give away our signals to a rival team."

Suddenly a strange glint came into Rachel's eyes and she looked intently at Seth. "What did you just say?" she asked.

"I said Billy Butler had to be lying," Seth repeated.

"No, not that," she persisted, "the part about Zach."

"All I said was Zach would never deliberately betray the Sluggers," said Seth. "He would never hurt us on purpose!"

"That's it!" cried Rachel. "That could explain everything!"

Both Andy and Seth looked at Rachel as if she had been out in the sun too long.

"What *are* you talking about?" asked Andy.

But Rachel didn't answer. She had turned her attention to the grandstand. Her eyes scanned the small crowd of spectators.

"There she is," Rachel said. "Thank goodness!"

"*Who?*" Seth demanded.

"Jennifer Barinski," Rachel replied.

Seth and Andy exchanged baffled looks.

"I thought we all agreed Jennifer couldn't be the sign stealer," said Andy.

"Of course, she isn't," said Rachel impatiently. "But she's the only one who can help us now."

"You better translate that one for us," said Seth. But Rachel was off into the stands. She climbed up to where Jennifer, wearing her red floppy hat, was sitting. Andy and Seth followed her.

"Jennifer?" said Rachel. "Hi! I'm Rachel Langlin."

"I know who you are," replied Jennifer brightly. "I've been watching you, and you're doing a great job in right field."

"Thanks," said Rachel. "Jennifer, I have to talk to you."

But just then Jennifer saw Seth standing next to Rachel. She immediately gave him her full attention.

"Seth!" Jennifer said. "Nice to meet you! Did Andy tell you how much I admire your playing?"

"He sure did," said Seth, grinning from ear to ear.

"Look Jennifer," broke in Rachel. "I'm sure Seth will be happy to share his fielding secrets with you after the game. But right now we need a favor."

"Sure. What is it?" asked Jennifer.

"When the inning's over, and we return to the field, I'd like you to stop watching Seth for a while," said Rachel. "I want you to focus your binoculars on my brother Zach instead."

Jennifer looked confused. "Okay! But why?" she asked.

"There's not enough time to explain," said Rachel. "But if my hunch is right, we'll soon know how our signs are being given to the Mudsharks."

"Are you serious?" Andy asked.

"You bet I am," replied Rachel. Then she turned back to Jennifer. "Well, what do you say? Can you do that and report to us about anything unusual that you see?"

"Don't worry," said Jennifer, catching some of Rachel's enthusiasm. "You can count on me!"

Suddenly a cheer went up from the people around them in the grandstand. Rachel and the others turned to the field and saw that Zach had just sliced a base hit over third and was standing on first base.

"What happened to our first batter?" Rachel called out to Susan Stein, sitting below on the bench.

"Out at first," said Susan. "What are you guys doing in the stands? Say, you didn't fall for that hogwash Billy Butler told us, did you?"

"I'll tell you about it later," Rachel said.

The inning was a good one for the Sluggers. Rachel hit what should have been a routine fly out. But, thanks to Mudshark errors, it turned into a stand-up double. This put Sluggers on second and third with one gone.

Marty came up to the plate next. The Mudshark pitcher got behind on a 3-balls, 1-strike count. Instead of risking a fat pitch down the middle, he purposely threw Marty a fourth ball. This loaded the bases and gave the Mudsharks a force out at every base. It was a good chance for a run-saving double play to get out of the inning.

Seth felt the pressure of batting with the bases loaded and one out. He took two strikes right over the plate. He was hoping the pitcher would still be a little wild and walk in a run.

Finally, Seth took an awkward chop at a low pitch and sent a high-bouncing grounder to the shortstop. The Mudsharks' fielder raced up for the ball, glanced at home, and then tossed underhand to third for the force out. That tied the score at 3–3 with two outs. The fourth inning ended when the next Slugger flied out.

The Sluggers took to the field with high spirits. Even Zach felt a little better. True, the Mudsharks still had the Sluggers' signals. But the Sluggers' fielding, led by Seth, Susan, and Rachel, kept things in check.

Three Mudsharks in a row waited for just the right pitch. All three knew exactly what the pitch would be and where Zach would put it. And all three hit long, powerful flies to the outfield that were caught for three outs.

As the Sluggers returned to the bench, Rachel raced

over to Jennifer, who had moved down to the first row in the grandstand.

"What did you see?" asked the rightfielder excitedly.

"At first, I wasn't sure," replied Jennifer. "But the longer I watched Zach, the more I realized he was doing it every time."

"Doing what?" Andy asked, approaching Rachel and Jennifer. Seth was right behind him.

"Sticking out his tongue!" exclaimed Jennifer. "He stuck out his tongue before every pitch!"

Seth looked disappointed. "He always does that," he said. "That's why we call him 'The Tongue.' "

"But he stuck it out a different way with each pitch," explained Jennifer.

"It's just as I suspected!" cried Rachel triumphantly. "Zach is giving away the pitch every time with his tongue! The signals had nothing to do with it!

"You mean nobody had to steal them?" asked Andy.

"Nope," replied Rachel. "All anybody had to do was watch what Zach did with his tongue. Then they'd know what every pitch would be!"

"Exactly!" said Jennifer. "I've been watching him the whole time. The position of his tongue changed from pitch to pitch. Here, I wrote it all down. I think I've figured out the code—if that's what you can call it."

Jennifer held out a scrap of paper for Rachel to read.

"It's amazing!" cried Andy. "Who would've ever thought it was possible."

"Jennifer, if you're as good a left fielder as you are a detective, you can play for the Sluggers anytime," said Rachel.

"And replace Seth?" exclaimed Jennifer. "No way!"

"You're okay, Jennifer," Seth smiled.

"Listen to this," Rachel said to her friends, when she had finished reading the paper. "According to Jennifer, Zach sticks his tongue out of the right side of his mouth before he pitches an inside ball. He pops his tongue out of the left side of his mouth when he's throwing an outside ball. He sticks his tongue straight up for a fastball. And he telegraphs every change-up by sticking his tongue straight down!"

Seth whistled loudly. "The Mudsharks must have figured it out during that last game we played against them," he said. "And then they passed the 'tongue signs' on to the Tigers and the Raiders."

"I feel like a fool," said Andy. "To think Zach's been sticking his tongue right out at me all this time. And I never realized it was giving away his pitches!"

"That's just it, Andy," said Rachel. "We were so used to seeing Zach stick out his tongue that we never paid any attention to it. The Mudsharks noticed it right away and put two and two together."

"So Billy Butler was telling the truth after all," said Andy. "But how did you ever guess, Rach?"

"It was when Seth said Zach would never *deliber-*

ately give away our signs," she replied. "It struck me that if he didn't deliberately give them away, he might have done it without knowing he was doing it. That was the only other possibility, if Billy wasn't lying. I suspected Zach's tongue was the giveaway, but I needed Jennifer and her binoculars to confirm it."

"This is great," said Jennifer. "But what are you going to do now that you know?"

"I'm going to have to bite off my tongue, I guess," said a familiar voice behind them.

It was Zach. He had been quietly standing there listening to every word.

"Zach!" exclaimed Rachel. "Then you know."

"Uh-huh," said her brother. "And if *you* feel like a fool, Andy, that makes me the prize dunce of all time."

"It's okay," said Andy. "Better we find out now than after the game."

"From now on, your tongue is staying put in your mouth—at least while you're pitching," Rachel said to her brother.

Zach thought about this for a moment. Then he looked at his friends and smiled. "No, Sis," he said. "I think I've got a better idea. . . ."

11 A Pitcher's Revenge

Rachel, Andy, Seth, and Jennifer stared at Zach.

"What do you mean, you have a better idea?" Rachel asked.

"I mean the Mudsharks did us a dirty trick," he explained. "So now I'm going to repay them the same way. I'm going to stick my tongue out just like before, but with a difference. This time, I'm going to change the pitches that go with each tongue position."

Rachel laughed loudly and threw her arms around her brother's neck. "I take back every nasty thing I've ever said or thought about you, Zach. You're a genius!"

"Guess it runs in the family," replied Zach with a grin.

"Okay, cut the gushy stuff," said Seth impatiently.

"Your idea's great, Zach. But what exactly is your plan?"

"Well," said Zach, rubbing his hands together. "If I always stuck my tongue out of the right side of my mouth before an inside pitch, now I'll do it before an outside pitch. Putting my tongue to the left side was an outside pitch. Now it'll come before a fastball down the middle of the plate. Sticking my tongue straight up will be a change-up instead of a fastball."

"Those Mudsharks will be so confused, they won't know what they're swinging at!" exclaimed Andy. "The way I see it, Zach, you won't need any pitching signals from me for this inning!"

"This is going to be a riot," said Jennifer. "I'm glad I have a front-row seat!"

While they were talking, the rest of the team was trying its best to break the tie. The Sluggers got two base hits, but couldn't bring in a run. Both the Mudsharks and Sluggers went scoreless in the fifth inning.

In the top of the sixth, Zach approached the mound slowly. He was concentrating on his false tongue signals. Zach was afraid he'd forget himself and go back to the real tongue signs by mistake.

The first batter up for the Mudsharks was Mike Moran. He was a poor hitter who usually swung on the first pitch. But, thanks to Zach's "tongue tell," Mike Moran had managed to get a couple of base hits earlier in the game. So now his confidence was really running high.

Zach eyed the batter carefully. Mike grinned back confidently. *He's just waiting for my tongue to tell him the pitch*, thought Zach. *Well, get ready for a surprise, pal.* As Zach slowly wound up for the pitch, he stuck his tongue out of the left side of his mouth.

Expecting an outside pitch, Mike started to lean his body into the plate. When the fastball zoomed in right down the middle, he was caught by surprise. Mike took a tight, wild swing that never got near the ball.

"Strike one!" cried the umpire.

Moran looked slightly bewildered. He stared at Zach strangely for a moment—then shook his head. Zach was tempted to smile, but he resisted. He didn't want to let the Mudsharks know what he was up to.

Mike spread his legs apart and prepared for the next pitch. This time, Zach slowly let his tongue protrude from the right side of his mouth. The batter looked pleased. He took a step back, tightened his grip on the bat, and brought it closer to his body. He was ready for the inside ball he thought was coming.

Zach threw an outside, hanging ball instead. Mike's tight swing fell way short of the inviting pitch.

"Strike two!" called the ump.

Mike Moran's dark eyes were filled with a mixture of anger and disbelief. Something was wrong, but he couldn't figure out exactly what it was.

Mike wiped beads of sweat from his face with the back of his hand and gritted his teeth. He pounded the plate a few times with his bat. Then he squared off. His eyes were alive with a desire to bash the next pitch.

Zach took his time. He let his tongue stick straight up from his mouth. Mike braced himself for a ripping fastball. But when the pitch came, it was a floater all the way. The batter swung quickly at the super-slow pitch. Then Mike just stood there as the umpire called out the last strike.

Mike Moran started to walk away, trailing his bat behind him. Then he turned for one last look at the pitcher. He expected Zach to be jumping up and down or rubbing it in. But Zach just gave him a faint smile. It was safe to say, Mike Moran was now totally confused.

This first out only slightly disturbed the Mudsharks. They didn't expect that much from Mike's bat anyway. But when their second batter, a stronger hitter, struck out just as quickly, they sensed something was very wrong.

The last batter up was none other than Billy Butler. Zach was definitely pleased. He had a score to settle with Billy. As for Billy, he looked worried. He knew all his team's hopes rested on his shoulders. He didn't like that one bit. But Billy tried to hide his uneasiness.

Billy smiled tensely at Zach and waved to someone in the stands. Zach decided he would have a little fun with Billy. He stuck his tongue straight out and then pulled it right back in. *Let's see what he makes of that*, Zach said to himself.

Poor Billy didn't know what to make of it. At first he thought maybe he was seeing wrong and Zach's tongue was actually pointing down. But when he looked again, he could see that it was gone. When the pitch came, Billy tried to keep his eye on the ball. But the fast outside pitch was totally unexpected. He fanned at the ball hopelessly with his bat.

A roar of laughter went up from the Slugger infielders. Billy glared at his rivals and pushed his glasses farther back on his nose.

"I'll fix you guys," he said grimly under his breath. Andy gave Zach the okay sign—one signal that even Mike Moran could have figured out.

Billy choked up on the bat, narrowed his eyes on the pitcher, and waited for the windup. But when Zach was ready to throw, Billy's eyes grew wide with amazement. Zach's tongue was jumping up, down, and side to side. It was all over the place. A fastball zipped over the plate and Billy's swing was wilder than before.

This time the laughter came from the grandstands. It was led by Jennifer. Billy Butler's round face turned as red as Jennifer's hat. He glared angrily up at the stands, at the Sluggers, but most fiercely of all at Zach Langlin.

As their eyes met, the pitcher could see that Billy knew exactly what was going on and was hopping mad about it. *Now you know what it feels like to be made a fool of,* thought Zach.

Billy beat the plate heavily with his bat, taking out all his frustrations on the piece of white rubber. Then he squared off with his bat, warming up his swing. He never took his eyes off the pitcher.

This time there'll be no tongue at all, you turkey, said Zach to himself. *Let's see how you handle that.* The pitch was slow and outside. Billy swung at it with his whole body. He swung so hard that his legs twisted together and he fell flat on his face.

"Three strikes! You're out!" cried the umpire.

"More like down and out!" cried Andy, laughing.

The fallen, defeated Mudshark got up from the ground, dusted himself off furiously, and stalked away. Zach couldn't resist. He stuck his tongue out at the departing Billy Butler.

The Sluggers trotted in for their last time at bat. The entire team was charged up by Zach's sixth-inning string of strikeouts. Coach Terwilliger greeted his pitcher with a big bear hug.

"That's my boy!" he cried. "Nice pitching!"

"Thanks, Coach," replied Zach. He didn't think it was the right time to tell him it was as much his tongue as his pitching arm that had struck out the Mudsharks.

"Well, we've put an end to the sign stealing," Rachel said to Seth. "Now we've just got to win this game."

"I think we can do it," said Seth. "Thanks to Zach."

By now, the Mudsharks knew that Zach had turned the tables on them. They were angry about it and were determined to come back and shut the Sluggers down in return.

The first batter up was Susan Stein. Susan was eager to prove herself to her teammates. When the pitcher threw a change-up, she surprised him with a bunt down the third-base line. She easily beat it out for a single.

"Way to go, Susan!" cried Rachel.

The Mudsharks' pitcher tried to overpower the next batter with fastballs. But Luis just stayed calm and waited him out. Sure enough, the fourth "fastball" came in with a lot less zip. Luis stroked a shot just over first base. This put Sluggers on first and second with nobody out.

Up came Andy to the plate. Andy was anxious to make up for some poor hitting in recent games. As usual, he swung with all his might on every pitch. After two mighty misses, he got lucky and sent a bullet past the shortstop for a single. The bases were now loaded.

Ernie Peters came up next and popped up to the pitcher for the Sluggers' first out. This put the game firmly in Zach's hands. A hit here of any kind would win it. But a double play could send the game into extra innings.

Zach was nervous. He knew he was an okay hitter — but no Seth Bradigan. Like all pitchers, Zach had to spend most of his practice time perfecting his pitching.

Zach tried not to think about that now. He knew the Sluggers needed one good hit to win the game. And Zach wanted to be the player to get that hit.

The Mudshark pitcher eyed the batter tensely. The pressure was on him too. He threw a fastball and Zach, eager to hit it, swung a second too soon.

"Strike one!" called out the umpire.

Zach took a deep breath and held it. Then he slowly let the air out of his lungs. This relaxed him and he squared off for the next pitch. The pitch was high and Zach let it go by.

"Ball one!" cried the ump.

The pitcher tugged down on his cap and dug one toe into the mound. If he walked Zach, it would bring Susan Stein home for the winning run. He had to strike Zach out.

He wound up slowly and threw an inside pitch. Zach's eye never left the spinning ball and the bat struck it solidly. The ball shot into the air toward right field. The Sluggers watched hopefully as the ball flew closer and closer to the foul line. It landed just outside it.

"Foul ball!" sang out the ump. "Strike two!"

A collective groan went up from the Slugger bench. Coach Terwilliger muttered something under his breath. Zach wiped his sweaty hands on his pants and gripped the bat.

The pitcher was taking no chances. He fell back on his best pitch—his fastball. The pitch was too close. Zach jumped back from the plate to avoid being hit.

"Ball two!" came the call.

The next pitch was high again. Zach nearly swung at it but pulled back at the last second.

"Ball three!"

This was it. The game could be riding on the next pitch. Zach could feel his heart pumping as he looked down at the plate and then up at the pitcher on the mound.

The pitcher was in no hurry. In that critical moment before the windup, Zach tried to guess what the fateful pitch would be. He knew the pitcher wouldn't risk a change-up that he could smack. That meant either a fastball or an inside ball. Zach knew the pitcher wouldn't walk him here. The fastball seemed more likely, but he couldn't be sure.

As he was thinking, the pitcher absentmindedly tugged at his cap again. Suddenly Zach knew exactly what he was going to throw. *The last time he did that, he threw an inside ball,* Zach thought. *If that's a "tell" like my tongue was, then the next pitch is going to be inside.*

Zach crouched down into his batting stance and hoped that his instincts were right. The pitcher wound up. The ball came swooping in toward the inside corner of the plate.

Zach was ready for it. He swung into the pitch—catching the ball squarely. Up, up it sailed, over second base, over the right fielder's head and over the fence surrounding Bloom Field. It was a grand slam!

For a moment Zach stood frozen, not believing what he had just done. Then the cries of his teammates broke the spell and he started to trot around the bases. As he rounded first he heard wild cheers at home plate. Susan Stein had reached home. When Zach rounded second, he caught a look of bitter disappointment on the face of the second baseman.

By the time Zach reached third, the cheers from the

Slugger fans had become a chant, "Zach! Zach! Zach!" Andy, Coach Terwilliger, and the rest of the Sluggers were waiting for him at home plate. Amid the congratulations, Zach cast a hurried glance up at the scoreboard. The final score was Sluggers 7, Mudsharks 3. The Sluggers had won!

The victory celebration at the Southside Ice Cream Shop was a memorable one. The entire team was there—as well as Jennifer Barinski, at Rachel's insistence.

Mr. Langlin served free ice cream to everyone. Coach Terwilliger was so happy that he agreed to forego his favorite flavor—vanilla—for a taste of Caramel Carrot Crunch. Even that didn't dampen his high spirits. As for Jennifer and Andy, they knew better than to ask for Mr. Langlin's latest flavor twice.

Rachel told the coach and her father how the signs had been given away to the Mudsharks. She also told them how she and Jennifer had learned the truth, and how Zach had finally turned the tables on Billy Butler and his teammates.

"Incredible!" exclaimed Coach Terwilliger. "You guys deserve a medal for this one. Although, personally I'd settle for the League Championship Trophy. It's like I always say—it takes more than guts and ability to play good baseball. You need brains, too!"

"Well," said Seth, sipping on the last of his strawberry shake. "Now that we've solved the mystery of

the stolen signs, I guess we won't have to worry about anybody stealing them again."

"Not as long as Zach keeps his tongue in his mouth," said Susan Stein, good-naturedly.

"Don't worry about that," said Zach. "I'll tie it in a knot before I give away another pitch."

Rachel laughed. "Now that's one thing I can't quite picture," she said.

"What's that?" asked Zach.

"You being tongue-tied!" replied his sister.

Everyone laughed at that, including Zach.

Coach Terwilliger's Corner

Hi there, all you Sluggers!

The signals a catcher gives to a pitcher are extremely important. They can help the pitcher strike out a batter by tailoring his or her pitches to the batter's weak points, while avoiding the strong ones. Signs are usually given by the catcher before each pitch. Most pitching signs are given with the fingers. Here are some basic signs you should know:

One finger pointed down— a fastball

Two fingers pointed down— a curveball

Three fingers pointed down— a change-up (slow ball)

Four fingers
pointed down —
a special pitch,
such as a knuckleball
or sinker ball

Wiggle of fingers
or a closed fist —
a pitchout (ball
pitched wide
of the plate)

To avoid a player or coach on the other team "stealing" a sign, the catcher should be very careful how he or she delivers them. Here are two ways to conceal your signs:

Put your mitt over your left knee. This will prevent the batter and the third-base coach from seeing your signs.

Keep your right knee slightly in front of your left knee. This will prevent the first-base coach from seeing your signs.

That's all for now. See you in the next Southside Sluggers Baseball Mystery. Until then, play ball!